MW00936867

Where's Eli Moore?

Discovering the Legend of the Amazon

ANNA HAGELE

Copyright © 2016 Anna Hagele

All rights reserved.

ISBN: 1535370513
ISBN-13: 978-1535370516

To my four wild adventurers -
Sam, Will, Michael, and Clare.

CONTENTS

ACKNOWLEDGMENTS

To Mom and Dad for starting off the journey.
To Jenny for always cheering me on.
To Josh for his imaginative ideas.
To Jess for always inviting me in.
To Peter for his prayers.
To Kathleen and Cordell for their generosity.
To Matt for being such an awesome uncle.
To Phyllis for being my second grandma.
To Mike, my partner in crime, for
FORMATTING - and also never giving up
on his scatter-brained wife.

1 GOING TO THE AMAZON?

I am finally going on my first expedition! My dad worked for weeks to get permission to hike into the Peruvian Amazon rainforest and he finally received approval. He's a biologist turned video blogger. He travels all over the world looking for interesting animals and makes videos about them. I've never gone on a trip with him before because I've been too young. But I just turned 10 and I convinced my parents that being a decade old had to come with certain perks, like hiking through the Amazon, for instance.

Dad was the first to come around. He's been going on his mini-expeditions for about five years and he's gotten really popular with his blogging. He's kind of a celebrity. All of my friends have watched his clips and some of them even get weird when they come over to the house. You know, like how people get when they meet someone who they see as "famous", kind of giggly and awkward. Not that I really mind it. I don't. I think Dad's job is, like, WAY COOL. The odd thing is he is not at all the celebrity type. I mean he's not super outgoing or good-looking. He is tall and thin with dark, square glasses. He doesn't have a very "shiny" personality. He's actually pretty quiet and sorta shy. Still, when he gets around an animal that he has never seen before, he gets really excited, sort of jumpy and bug-eyed. He fumbles over his words and shifts his glasses and clears his throat a lot. Not exactly the super-video-blogger-type, but I think that's what people like about him. He's just an ordinary, scientist-type guy who is REALLY enthusiastic about animals and about teaching other people about them.

So, as you can imagine, it wasn't that hard to convince Dad to take along his only son on an expedition to share some of that enthusiasm. To be fair, I am almost as nuts about animals as he is. I have read just about everything I can about them, encyclopedias full of animal facts and figures. I also have kept a pretty decent field journal over the past three years of all of the animals I have found around our yard, neighborhood and town. We live in Flagstaff, Arizona, which is a high altitude mountain town about an hour from the Grand Canyon. I am particularly proud of my drawings and notes on the Abert's squirrel, or tassel-eared squirrel, that lives in one of the high-reaching pine trees in our front yard. Its Latin name is Sciurus aberti and I have observed it almost every day for the past few months. When I showed my journal to Dad, he got really excited and started aiding me in my efforts to convince my mom that I should go along with him on his next trip.

"Why does it have to be the Amazon?" Mom said, her arms firmly crossed in front of her. We were all standing in the kitchen after dinner. My mom had turned from the sink, her arms still soapy from dishwater.

"I know, I know. It sounds big and wild and intimidating," my dad said, turning to place a dinner plate in the cupboard, almost hitting his forehead on the light fixture.

"You are not helping," Mom interjected.

"Right. So, we won't be going deep into the forest. We will be looking for a little lizard called a dwarf dragon. We will go on a day trip or maybe for just one night in the jungle plus a few travel days," he said.

"You are going to take our 10-year-old son into the Amazon jungle overnight?" she said, her voice rising and her arms dropping.

"Mom, please! Dad will be with me the whole time and I am sure he wouldn't take me anywhere super dangerous. Besides, we will have Kara with us," I said. At the mention of her name, our German Shepherd came padding into the kitchen, looking at me expectantly. She is an unusual dog. She doesn't look like most German Shepherds, either red and black or tan and black, because she has a sable coat, black and gray, which gives her an uncanny resemblance to a gray wolf. She is also very intelligent. I mean I know every kid thinks that their dog is really smart, but Kara is different. Dad takes her on all of his trips and he always comes home with a story of how she saved him from this snake or that animal or from the 20 foot drop that absent-minded Dad just happened to not see coming. Mom always says that Kara is the reason Dad is still alive. But when Dad comes home, Kara is definitely my dog. I feed her and she sleeps in my bed every night. Mom says that Kara knows the exact time that my school bus comes in the afternoons. At 3:15 every weekday, Kara slips out the dog door and sits on the front porch just in time for my bus's 3:20 arrival.

That night in the kitchen, when we were trying to convince Mom, Kara came and sat by me, cocking her head up at Mom with a questioning look in her eyes.

"Ugh! Not you too!" Mom said to Kara, exasperated. "I am outnumbered by the three of you adventurers!" Eventually, she did give in and not in the least because Kara was going along on the trip. As tall and awkward as Dad is, Mom is soft and warm. She is much shorter than Dad and plump in the best way. She is soulful and kind and protective. Everything about her is comfortable except perhaps for her sharp mind, quick as steel. I look like Dad, tall and thin with glasses. Mom says both Dad and I are wild and wiry.

Now here I am, the morning of our expedition. Our first flight will leave from Phoenix and, then, numerous connections later, we will arrive in Lima, the capital of Peru. Just before I climb into Dad's dark blue, four-door Kia, I turn to give Mom one last hug. She has tears in her eyes. I suddenly feel sorry and guilty for leaving her this way, alone and worried, but her tears are intermixed with a proud smile.

"Listen to your dad and pay attention to

Kara. Most of all, listen to yourself, Eli. May your path be straight and may light always shine upon you," she says. I hug her tight, trying not to cry myself, and then slide into the backseat. As we drive up onto the highway, excitement pumps through my chest. I am really going! Onward to the Amazon!

2 EL LOBO

The next 36 hours are a blur of plane flights and airports. Our first stop is in Boston, Massachusetts and then in Fort Lauderdale, Florida. I haven't done much traveling so I'm not sure what to expect, but the airports in those two cities are pretty much like the Phoenix airport. Kara has to ride in a cargo kennel the whole way, which makes Dad really nervous because we don't get to see her until we finally land in Lima. Now, let me tell you, when we do land in Lima, things are different, way different. I mean, we are definitely no longer in the United States. The people in the Lima airport all speak Spanish and the air immediately feels heavier, even inside. We pick up our checked luggage and then head over to be reunited with Kara. The airport staff quickly finds her kennel and allows us to release her. When she comes out, she looks sleepy and stiff, but perks up as soon as she sees Dad and me. The airport staff gives her a wide berth and one man whispers, "El lobo!" We walk through the airport to our next connection and other people look uncomfortably at Kara and more of them say the words, "El lobo."

"What does 'el lobo' mean, Dad?" I ask.

"Ah, yes. It means wolf. I find that lots of people in other countries are a bit uncomfortable with Kara's appearance," he explains.

"You mean they think she is actually a wolf?" I ask.

"Yeah or part wolf," Dad says.

"But if you just look at her carefully, you can see that she is a German Shepherd," I say.

"Well, many people are not that familiar with German Shepherds. The world is a very big place, Eli, and depending on the corner of it in which you find yourself, a dog can be a wolf," he says. "Come this way! We have one flight left. A small charter will take us to Iquitos. From there, we will take a boat down the Amazon River to our outpost." Dad points to the left. I am surprised at how calm he seems amidst all of the stares and comments from the other people in the airport. I guess he's used to it, but I'm not. I mean we get looks back home sometimes when we have Kara with us, but not like this. Of course, it is weird to see a dog of any sort walking through an airport, not to mention one that looks like Kara. My face burns with embarrassment and I decide to look at my feet the rest of the way to the charter plane.

Kara — "El Lobo"

We walk out onto a ramp outside of the airport and the air sticks to my skin. I am used to the high, dry air of northern Arizona. This air is like walking into soup! We approach a very small, silver plane that looks like it can hold maybe four or five passengers at best. A little, thin man comes out from behind one of its wings.

"Hello, Peter!" the man says, reaching out his hand to Dad. The man has a broad, white smile that breaks through his straight, thin face. I would guess he is about Dad's age or maybe a little younger. He obviously knows Dad.

"Gabriel! It's so good to see you! I want to introduce you to my son, Eli," Dad says, gesturing to me.

"Hello, Eli, Peter's son! It is good to meet you," Gabriel says, shaking my hand vigorously. I nod to him, suddenly feeling shy. His voice has a funny inflection, full of rolling r's and odd vowels, much like other Spanish accents that I have heard, yet somehow different. I like it and want him to talk again.

"Gabriel works at the outpost where we will be stationed in the forest. He is a ranger and helps with conservation. He has seen our elusive dwarf dragon lizard. He will go with us on the next part of our trip," Dad says. I nod again.

"And there is the real explorer! Hello, Kara!" Gabriel says, greeting Kara with a clap and a pat on the back. She barks in reply and then allows her head to be massaged, her tongue lolling out of her mouth.

"Are you ready, then?" Gabriel asks. Dad nods and we pull our luggage up the stairs of the little plane. Kara lies down by my feet. She gets to ride in the cabin for this flight. My heart skips a beat as we buckle ourselves in. So far, we have only flown on the big planes. I brace myself for takeoff as Gabriel sits in the cockpit and fires up the engine. The roar of it is loud and open. I can feel the rumbling of its power in my belly. As we take off, the push of gravity against my body is very strong and the shift of the plane as it rights itself in the air feels like a roller coaster ride. Finally, we are up, soaring high above the city of Lima. It is late afternoon and the light of the sun shines full on the rows of buildings below us. Soon, the city gives way to an ocean of green and my mind fills with the idea of all that lies below, the teeming, thriving, throbbing life of the jungle.

"Look, Dad! It's there! It's right below us!" I yell over the engine. Dad laughs.

"I know, right? Pretty unbelievable, huh?" he says. The plane ride is pretty quick, just over an hour, and Gabriel lands at the airport in Iquitos, Peru just as the sun begins to set.

"We will stay here tonight and then take the boat in the morning," Gabriel says as we get off the plane. He hails a taxi outside of the airport. The driver is tentative at first, not sure if he wants to allow "el lobo" to ride in his taxi, but eventually comes around when Dad offers him an extra tip. We climb into the car and zip along the streets of Iquitos. I am surprised to see how big of a city it is. I mean it is totally surrounded by jungle, cut off from most of the rest of the world, and yet its streets move and pulse much like the streets of an American city. Still, as the evening streetlights and storefront glows come to life, all seems strange and bright to me. The whole city feels more colorful and wilder than anywhere I have ever been, almost like the jungle surrounding it has leaked into the city itself, making it more alive somehow. The taxi stops in front of a hotel and we get out. The hotel is a deep red adobe and has curves and arches all over it that remind me of a bullfighter's outfit. We walk into the lobby to check in and I suddenly feel very hungry and tired. My stomach is edgy and jumpy from all the plane rides and the lack of a full night's sleep. I sit down on a brown leather chair while Dad talks with someone at the front desk. Kara sits next to me and lets out a soft whine, lying her head on my lap. She's hungry, too.

"Okay! Let's get some food and some sleep!" Dad says, walking over to me, pulling me up to a standing position by the straps of my backpack.

The food at the hotel is strange, but delicious. They have these meatball things made from pork and crushed plantains (which are like bananas) that are amazing. I could eat like twenty of them. They also have this rice, chicken and egg ball that's pretty good. After we eat, we go up to the hotel room and I pass out happily on a bed next to Dad with Kara sleeping at my feet. I feel so tired I think I could sleep for a week, but I am looking forward to tomorrow. That's when the real adventure begins. First off, a boat ride on the Amazon River!

3 IT'S REALLY PINK!

The morning dawns overcast and hazy. I walk out of the hotel and am once again struck by the thick, humid air. We take another taxi over to the river port. As I get out of the cab, the smell of earthy water hits me and then I see it! The Amazon River! It is brown and blue, winding through the forest like a python. There is a long, low motor boat waiting in the water just off the bank. Two men are already sitting in it. One of them is seated by the motor and has a uniform shirt on saying something about tours. I realize he must be our driver and guide while we are on the river. The other man is very small and very old. He has dark, wrinkled skin and a shock of short, white hair on his head that reminds me of a Q-tip. He turns to me and looks at me with sharp eyes and then smiles. Three or four of his teeth are missing and I look up at Dad with a question in my eyes. Who is this crazy, old guy and are we sure we want to ride down the Amazon River with him?

"Papa!" Gabriel says, climbing onto the boat and embracing the old man. "Peter! Eli! This is my father, Juan Carlos. He is visiting me from my home in the mountains. He will be coming with us on the river today and will stay at the outpost with me for some time. He only speaks Spanish," he says.

"Hola, Senor," Dad says. He can speak a little Spanish and does his best to say something that makes sense. Juan Carlos nods and smiles his weird grin.

Soon, we are all loaded onto the boat with our gear. Kara sits next to my bench. Old Juan Carlos is obviously uncomfortable with Kara in the boat and moves quietly to the opposite side. Kara is well-trained though, and, as I said before, unusually intelligent. She knows not to jump in the water after some animal. She is still, but very alert, sitting straight up, her head cocked as the boat engine bursts to life and pushes us out onto the water. We start off fast, the rush of the air and spray from the river hitting my face.

Then we slow down as we reach the main current of the river and allow it to carry us downstream, away from Iquitos. We are soon surrounded on all sides by green jungle.

"So, you will be looking for caiman and the pink river dolphin. They are sometimes here in this part of the river where the current is strong," says the guide. His name is Jose and his accent is very thick. I have to concentrate to understand him over the sound of the motor.

"Good, good!" Dad says. He is starting to get excited and keeps checking the camera that he has strung around his neck.

"I know the main event is the dwarf dragon, but I want to make sure we get everything else!" he says to me. Then he takes the camera off and turns it toward himself.

"Well, this is it! We are riding down the Amazon River! We are going to search for the newly discovered dwarf dragon. As I have told you in previous clips, my son, Eli, is coming with me this time." He turns the camera in my direction and I wave. "And, of course, Kara is along for the ride as well," Dad says, pointing the camera at Kara who looks over at him with an almost practiced dog grin. Everyone loves Kara. She is almost more famous than Dad.

The camera is soon slung around his neck again so that it can catch all that we see as we travel. Dad will edit it after the trip, tweak it, cut it and add little funny sound effects.

We enter into a faster part of the river and Jose lowers the speed of the motor even further. Suddenly, he points in front of us to the left.

"There! Yes! River dolphins! They have been swimming there lately!" he says.

"What? Where?" I ask. I almost stand up in the boat to get a better look, but then think better of it. I look up the river, searching for what Jose's eyes have already spotted. Then I see it! Something moving up over the surface of the water, sleek and rose-colored. Then I see it again! Something is definitely jumping up out of the water. As we get closer, my eyes focus in and I can clearly see the smooth, pink body of the river dolphin and its back fin as it jumps up out of the water. And then another one! And another one!

"Wow! Look at them! Do you see them?" I say. Kara is standing in the boat now and barks a couple of times at the jumping dolphins. We all laugh at her. "Can you see them, girl? Wow, they really are pink!" I exclaim and then everyone laughs at me. Dad gets some good footage of the dolphins and then explains to the camera that their Latin name is Inia geoffrensis. He tells his viewers that, just like dolphins living in the ocean, the river dolphins are mammals and must come up to the surface periodically for air. He also talks about the fish, shrimp and crabs that they eat. In only a moment, we pass by the pink, jumping mammals of the Amazon River and my heart is full. I take out my field journal and do a rough sketch, but only for a few minutes. I don't want to miss anything on our journey.

Pink River Dolphin — Inia Geoffrensis

Pink color is really amazing!
We saw three of them leaping
out of the water.

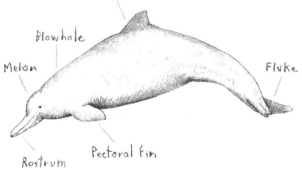

Dorsal Fin

Blowhole

Melon

Fluke

Rostrum

Pectoral Fin

We travel down the river for the next four hours, eating our lunch in the boat. Dad brought dried fruit and nuts along with some beef jerky for us to munch on. We see lots of jungle birds flying from one side of the river to the other and the shadows of fish swimming in the depths. Other than that, our first, lucky view of the river dolphin is the only wildlife we see. The river all on its own is pretty incredible though. It is so large and quick and brown that it feels like an animal itself. In the late afternoon, we finally come up to an open bank on the right side of the river. Jose waves goodbye and turns his boat around to travel back up the current.

4 A BLUE MORPHO AND LOUD MR. JOHNSON

"It will take about an hour to hike to the outpost," Dad says to me as we stand on the edge of the river.

"Do you think we will see anything else on the way there?" I ask.

"Maybe, if we pay attention. As you know, the forest is full of animal life, but it can be elusive," Dad says. I put my field journal into my pack, but place it on top in case I need to pull it out quickly. The first thing I notice as we leave the rush of the river is an odd droning sound that surrounds us. I realize quickly that it is from the tons of bugs that are in the rainforest. With every step I take I can feel and see little bugs everywhere, crawling and flying and wiggling their way through the forest! Even though I am totally thrilled about finally being in the rainforest, my creepy-crawly, heeby-jeeby sense starts to take over. I feel jumpy and itchy and sort of like I want to swat the whole jungle with a giant flyswatter, just to clear it out a bit. I can tell that Kara feels kind of the same way as she keeps sneezing every once in a while, her sensitive nose adjusting to the smells and bugs of the forest. The smell of the forest is also intense. It reminds me of walking into a greenhouse, only heavier and denser. It smells like soil and rain and plants mixed with flowers and damp bark. The forests back at home in Phoenix are pine and have that fresh, minty smell. Here, the smell is heavy with water and heat and life. It is also much darker than I expected under the canopy of trees. Even during the day, there is this shadowy, husky feeling to the light because the trees don't actually let in that much direct sunlight. Not that it isn't hot because, boy, is it ever! From the moment we step off the boat and walk away from the river, sweat trickles down my face and back.

While we walk, I suddenly see a flash of blue to my right.

"Dad! What's that?" I ask. We all stop

and turn. Dad half walks, half runs over to a tree whose trunk is about as wide as a small car.

"Look! It's a blue morpho butterfly, a Morpho peleidas. Look at that shade of bright blue!" he says, holding his camera to the butterfly.

"Wow! It's bigger than I thought it would be!" I say. I have read about the blue morpho, but nothing compares to seeing it up close in real life. The top of it is a brilliant shade of blue while its underside is brown with eye spots. When it flies, it gives the illusion that it is appearing and disappearing, flapping between bright blue and brown. It does this to confuse predators. I pull out my journal and quickly sketch it, careful not to disturb it as I copy its intricate underwing pattern of eyespots. Dad finishes getting some good footage and making his commentary while Juan Carlos and Gabriel wait patiently on the trail. Kara sneezes again and then lies down.

Blue Morpho Butterfly - Morpho Peleides

farewing

Antenna

hindwing

Wing veins

Beautiful blue color. Edges black, white, and red

Antenna

Compound eyes

Eye spots

Eye spots help to camouflage. Butterfly seems to appear and then disappear as it flies, confusing predators.

Dad and I finish up our examination of the blue morpho and we all start hiking again. Now that the excitement of the butterfly is over, my creepy-crawlies are back and I am relieved when we get to the outpost. It's not much, just a few crudely built huts with thatched roofs surrounding a main fire pit. It is located in a natural clearing, an island of open ground amidst the sea of forest canopy. There are a few other travelers already staying at the outpost. One of them, a short, wide American man, older than my father but not as old as Juan Carlos, comes over to us as soon as we enter the clearing.

"Hi, ho, there! My name is William Henry Johnson the third! Welcome to our Amazon outpost!" he says very loudly, shaking hands with Dad and giving me a wink.

"Mr. Johnson, how was your hike yesterday?" Gabriel asks.

"Fine, fine! Nothing really to report though, in terms of ruins," he says.

"Mr. Johnson is an archeologist. He believes that there may be some overlooked Inca ruins in this part of the forest," Gabriel explains.

"How interesting!" Dad says.

"Mr. Johnson, this is Peter Moore. He is a biologist who makes videos for children about animals from all over the world," Gabriel says.

"Ah! You use the Internet then or computers somehow?" Mr. Johnson asks. But before Dad can answer, he comes over to me.

"My goodness! Is this your boy? Brave lad to come hike the Amazon with his dad! And who is this?" he asks, noticing Kara.

"That's Kara, our dog," I say.

"She is a beauty! German Shepherd?' he asks.

"Yes," I say.

"But such unusual coloring! Come here, girl!" Mr. Johnson says, roughly shaking Kara's head, petting her far too hard. I wince as he does it because I can tell that Kara is irritated. She shakes herself away from loud Mr. Johnson and walks off towards one of the huts, obviously feeling like her dignity has been compromised. Mr. Johnson then turns to me again and for a moment I think he is going to rub my head as hard as he did Kara's. Instead, he slaps me on the back so hard that my glasses slip down my nose. I smile and try to answer his loud questions for a while, but then slink off much like Kara did toward the other side of the outpost. I feel a little treacherous as loud Mr. Johnson moves on to

Dad, slapping him on the back as hard as he did me. I find Kara who is sitting at the edge of the outpost, staring out into the forest.

"Hey, girl! I noticed they are starting the fire. I bet supper will be ready soon," I say to her, kneeling beside her, my hand on her back. She looks at me for a moment and then back out at the forest. I look with her. The first few trees on the edge of the clearing are large and tall, like guards. Beyond them, I can see more tree trunks standing and some underbrush. Beyond that, however, there is little to see, only a deep green shadow that churns and moves somehow. My curiosity and sense of adventure rise within me. What lies within? What makes the green shadow seem to move? The cicadas begin to whir, throbbing loudly through the forest broken by the sharp cry of a bird somewhere high in the canopy. Another feeling begins to echo around inside of me, a small whisper of uncertainty, of fear. The immensity of the forest is alarming, the simple bigness or it - far, far bigger than one 10-year-old boy. Kara looks away from the forest and back to me. She lets out a small whine and licks my face. Her wet, rough tongue tickles.

"All right, girl. I'm all right," I say. "It's just a little spooky. Come on, let's go get some dinner," I say. We both turn around facing the newly started fire, our backs to the jungle.

5 THE LEGEND OF EL TUNCHI (AHHHH!)

We all sit around the fire, the rangers, the tourists, loud Mr. Johnson, old Juan Carlos, Dad, Kara and me. The rangers cook up pork and chicken for us along with some plantains and I dig in. Kara especially likes the pork and is soon snoozing beside me as the night deepens around us. As the darkness grows, the movements and noises from the jungle around us get wilder and weirder. Strange, echoing calls accompany shifts and movements in the trees.

"Sounds like there's a troop of howler monkeys nearby. They make quite a racket," Gabriel says, explaining the strange calls and movement.

"Could we see one?" I ask Dad.

"Probably not a good idea to go out and find a troop like that at night, Eli. They can be territorial," Dad answers. I nod, sort of relieved that we aren't going out into the jungle tonight.

After dinner, everyone sits around the fire talking and laughing and telling stories. A few people decide to leave the fire for their hut and Gabriel goes with them to help them find their way in the dark. Dad is having fun entertaining a couple of tourists who have seen some of his blogs online. He is telling them about the time he almost got bitten by a funnel web spider in Australia when, all of a sudden, old Juan Carlos raises his voice above the others.

"Escucha! Escucha!" he says in Spanish. Loud Mr. Johnson is sitting next to him and translates to the rest of us.

"He says, 'Listen! Listen!'" Evidently loud Mr. Johnson knows how to speak Spanish. Old Juan Carlos begins to talk in a chant like voice, rocking back and forth.

"He says that he wants to tell us about a jungle story, an old legend from his people. The jungle is like a mother to us. She gives us all we need to survive, but if we are cruel to her creatures or take more than we need, she can be harsh and unforgiving. Mother Jungle also has no patience for fools who come to her unprepared." Dad looks over at me, raises an eyebrow, and turns his forefinger in a circle near his ear making a "cuckoo" gesture. I suppress a laugh.

"In the midst of the jungle, there is an ancient spirit who roams through the trees. El Tunchi he is called. He is the spirit of all those who have died or been lost in the jungle. He seeks out those who wish to harm Mother Jungle or who are foolish. You will know him by the sound that he makes, a low, clear whistle with three tones." Loud Mr. Johnson stops for a moment as old Juan Carlos holds up three fingers and begins speaking again.

"If you hear the whistle, you know that El Tunchi is close by. When you hear the whistle, you will have a terrible temptation to repeat it. But you must not answer his tune. If you do, he will come and either terrorize you or take you deep into the jungle, a lost soul, just like him!" At the end of this sentence, old Juan Carlos sits down heavily. Everyone is quiet for a full beat. Then loud Mr. Johnson says,

"Boogedy, boogedy, boo!" Everyone laughs except for old Juan Carlos who glares at old Mr. Johnson. I also do not laugh, but place my hand on Kara's back. She sits up, suddenly aware of me and the others, looking around for danger. Dad laughs only half-heartedly and walks over to me, placing his hand on my shoulder.

"All right then, enough ghost stories for tonight. We have a big day ahead of us. Come on, Eli, Kara!" he says. The others tell us goodnight and Dad leads me to our hut.

"Don't pay any attention to that story, Eli. It's just an old legend, been around the Amazon for generations," he says, trying to make me feel better.

"Yeah, it's okay, Dad. I mean I know there are no such things as spirits. El Tunchi! Ha!" I say this unconvincingly. Dad smiles and puts his arm around me.

"Get some sleep and keep Kara close by. I'm in the bed right next to yours if you need anything," he says.

Soon I am lying in my bed, which is really just a flat pad on the floor of the hut. Mosquito netting is hung all around it. Kara tucks in near my feet beneath the net and I lie down, waiting to fall asleep. I know that the story of El Tunchi is not real, yet my mind goes back to the dark green shadows of the forest and the idea of a spirit moving through the depths of the jungle suddenly does not seem so farfetched. I try to think of other things, of the blue morpho we saw and the pink river dolphin. I try to think of the elusive dwarf dragon lizard that we will search for tomorrow. Still, my mind is always drawn back to the haunted spirit with his three-toned whistle. Sometime after midnight, I finally fall asleep, whistles and a man with long, white fingers slipping into my dreams.

6 THE CAT-MOUSE

The next day dawns clear and mild. The sky is blue through the clearing, but there is always a humid haze over the jungle, which tints the sky. The dreams and stories of the night before feel long ago and I am ready for the hike.

"Maybe we will see one of those howler monkeys!" I say to Kara as I get dressed. She picks up on my excitement and we both run out of the hut to find Dad. He is over in the main ranger station with Gabriel going over some final maps.

"I have seen a few of them in this area, so I think that is going to be your best shot," Gabriel says, pointing at a spot about 10 miles from the outpost.

"And the trail goes right by there?" Dad

asks.

"Yes. I have seen many while I am walking, especially in the evenings and mornings," Gabriel replies.

"Great! Ah, Eli! Good morning! Would you like to take a look at the map?" Dad asks.

"Sure!" I say, stepping up to the map which is spread out over a wooden desk. I love maps. This one is a topographical map, which is difficult to read, but Gabriel points out to me where the outpost is and the area where we are headed.

"So, we are going northwest of the outpost?" I ask.

"Yes. The trail will lead you there. I just walked it a week ago and everything was clear," Gabriel says.

"Right. We will walk there today, arriving early this afternoon. We will set up camp and then spend the evening looking for dwarf dragons. Then we will stay the night in camp and look again for the lizards in the morning if we have not found any by then. Finally, we will break camp and be back to the outpost by tomorrow evening," Dad says.

"That is the plan. Should be simple. The weather is supposed to be clear and there have been no jaguar sightings in the area for some time. They head deeper into the jungle during the winter," Gabriel explains. I jump inwardly a little at the mention of jaguars, but I am also very excited to see the dwarf dragons.

"Okay! When do we leave?" I ask.

"As soon as we eat some breakfast and check our gear!" Dad says.

Within the hour, Gabriel is waving us goodbye and we are headed off on the trail. I have the same creepy-crawly feeling that I did yesterday, but it's not as bad. My mind is adjusting to the idea that there are little bugs crawling everywhere and, after about a half hour of hiking, I don't notice it much anymore. We walk on, finding a steady pace. I am actually used to this part of hiking—the slow hours of walking on a trail with a pack on your back. We go hiking a lot back in Arizona. Still, the rainforest is different. The trees are so tall and large that I feel like I've been shrunk or maybe found my way into a land of giants.

We stop to rest after about two hours and have some water and energy bars. Dad spots a funny little creature called an agouti that looks like a large mouse with no tail. We stay very still and Dad is able to get some footage of it, whispering his commentary. Agoutis are very shy around humans and usually run away and hide. We get lucky and are able to watch this one for some time until Kara decides that it is just too much like a small cat or a squirrel to leave alone. She barks at it and runs after it as it flies into the forest.

"Kara! Come!" Dad says. Kara immediately turns from the "small cat" and comes back to us, her eyes shining. Dad laughs at her and brings the camera up to her happy face.

Agouti - Dasyprocta

This guy was really cute!
Kara thought he was a little cat

Rounded body / back

There is a tail
but it is tiny!

Small round ears

Big eyes

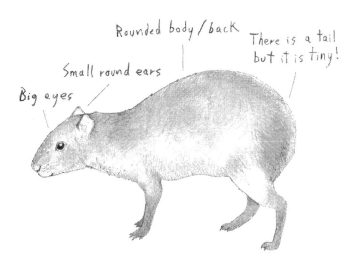

"Why'd you scare it away, Kara? Huh?" he asks. Kara barks again, this time playfully at Dad, and then we start back on the trail. At half past 1:00, Dad stops. He looks at the ground underneath a tree with an enormous trunk.

"What do you see?" I ask.

"Nothing," Dad says and smiles. "That's good. I think we should set up camp here beside this large tree trunk; I don't want any big colonies of ants living underneath us," he says.

"Oh! Are we here, in the area where Gabriel saw the dwarf dragons?" I ask.

"I think we are pretty close. They usually don't come out until sunset, so we should have enough time to set up the tent and get some firewood," Dad says. He begins to unroll the lightweight tent from his pack and I help him stand it up and tie it to some tree roots. We put the rest of our gear inside the tent.

"Let's find some stones to make a fire ring and then some wood," Dad says. We search around the campsite and soon find some rocks. Dry wood is harder to find as everything in the forest seems to be constantly soaked with moisture. Not far from the camp, however, we find a downed tree that is dry in the middle. Dad brought along his knife and is able to cut off some twigs and good chunks of wood from the dead trunk. I help him carry the wood back to the fire circle.

"Okay, we will start the fire after we hunt for the dwarf dragons. I don't want to scare them away with it. Let's be still for a little while, drink some water, and see what we can see," Dad says.

7 A DRAGON!

We sit for almost an hour. I spend some time on my field journal, filling in my sketches of both the pink dolphin and the blue morpho butterfly. I also work on a new sketch of the agouti. Dad cleans and examines his camera gear, making sure that everything is ready in case we see the lizard. Kara passes out on the ground next to me, sleeping so heavily that she begins to snore. Finally, towards evening, Dad stands up.

"Okay, let's start to scout around the camp a little. Remember, be quiet with slow movements and stay together. Kara! Shhhht!" Dad makes this sound to Kara only when he wants her to go into stealth mode. I have to fight not to break up laughing because Kara suddenly crouches low to the ground, slowly sliding along the ground shifting her hips back and forth. She looks like a strange cat—a dog-cat! I look away from her to keep from laughing and instead focus on the forest around me. Dwarf dragons are also called wood dragons and I look for any downed tree trunks that might provide a hiding place. I also look for any sudden quick movement. That is tricky because, once you really focus in on it, the rainforest seems to have sudden quick movements all over the place, especially because of the bugs. I come across a colony of leaf-cutter ants and watch them for a moment, mentally noting the way they move and carry leaves so that I can sketch it later in my field journal.

We do this stealth walk for the next half hour without any sign of a dwarf dragon. Finally, just as the light begins to fade, Dad whispers my name. "Eli! Over there!" He points to a downed tree not far in front of us. At first I can't see it, but as my eyes focus in on the trunk, I notice a small, triangular, green head peeking up over the trunk. Dad starts filming immediately, but then gestures to me to come closer to him. He takes off the camera from around his neck and hands it to me. He very carefully moves towards the log. Kara completely stops. She and I are as still as statues. Dad leaps awkwardly, but surprisingly quickly, at the log and comes up with a five inch green lizard in his hands. He is grinning from ear to ear. Although much smaller than a dragon, it totally looks like one with a spine running down the length of its back and long, finger-like claws on its feet. Its underbelly is white and it has a black and white ring around its neck.

"Look! Look! Can you believe it? We found it! A green dwarf dragon lizard! Enyalioides altotambo, also known as a wood lizard! This beautiful little lizard is a relatively newly discovered species. In recent years, there have actually been three different variations of this lizard found in Ecuador and Peru, each its own species. The diversity of life in the Amazon is amazing. It is thought by biologists that deep in the rainforest there are still many more new species of plants and animals for us to discover. Here, Kara! Have a look!" Dad says, holding the frightened lizard down toward Kara who immediately comes over to sniff the little guy. The dwarf dragon hisses angrily in response to Kara's sniff. Kara quickly steps away, her head cocked to one side in curiosity, and then barks at the little, hissing creature. Both Dad and I laugh.

"Well, that's about it for our trip through the Amazon looking for dragons—dwarf dragons, that is. Until next time, Kara and I as well as Eli say, 'Smell ya later!'"

Dwarf Dragon – Enyalioides Altotambo

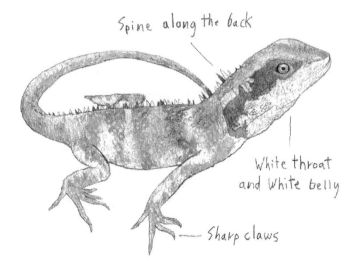

Spine along the back

White throat
and white belly

Sharp claws

There have been three new species
of dwarf dragons found recently in
Peru and Ecuador.

About 4 to 5 inches long.

Dad lets the hissing dwarf dragon go and it scampers quickly under the fallen log. We walk back to the campsite. Dad and I talk a mile a minute while we get the fire started. I can tell that Dad is relieved that we found the dwarf dragon—that was the hook for his blog. We cook up some premade kabobs that Dad and Gabriel made early this morning and head into the tent. The long hike and excitement of finding the dwarf dragon drove any fears I had about El Tunchi right out of my mind. I fall asleep quickly, listening to the already familiar throb of the cicadas echoing through the rainforest.

8 A WHISTLE IN THE NIGHT

I wake up suddenly, sitting straight up. It is in the middle of the night. Kara and Dad are still asleep. I listen for a moment. The cicadas have stopped their singing and the birds are quiet. There are strange deep gulping noises that I think are frogs. Something woke me up though, a sound. I am still. I listen harder. There are other noises too, quiet movements on the ground and shifting in the trees above, but nothing that sounds close. Just when I am about to lay down and go back to sleep, I hear it—a low, clear whistle. I freeze. Maybe it's just the wind moving through the leaves or a hollow place in a trunk. It was only one tone. Then it comes again, only this time in a higher tone. My heart starts to pound. Finally, a third tone, this one lower than the first two. My belly drops and I start shaking. I pound Dad on his arm.

"Dad! Dad!" I half whisper, half yell to him. He sits up with a start.

"What? What is it?" he asks, still half asleep.

"Dad!" I whisper-yell to him again, not able to tell him what I had heard. I am still hitting him on the arm.

"Eli! Stop hitting me! What is the matter?" Dad says, shaking my shoulders gently. Kara is up now as well and is sitting beside me.

"I heard … I heard…" I say.

"What? What did you hear? Did you hear a growl?" Dad asks. He grabs his glasses and looks at me. He obviously suspects that I might have heard a jaguar and he looks at Kara to see if she seems nervous. But Kara sits calmly beside me, looking at me with the same questioning look that Dad has on his face.

"I heard … three … whistles." I say this last part in a whisper, emphasizing three with my fingers. Dad breaks out laughing.

"What? Eli … oh, Eli!" After his initial laughter, Dad gives me a hug.

"It's okay, buddy, but really there is no

such thing as El Tunchi. It is a myth. You must have dreamed it or maybe heard an unusual frog or something," he says. "Now, go back to sleep, okay?" I nod. I don't have the energy or courage to argue with him. We all lay back down, but my eyes stay wide open. There is no way I am going back to sleep. I know I heard a whistle in three tones.

The rest of the night goes by very slowly for me. I listen to all of the jungle noises around me, waiting for another whistle. But none comes. I hear everything but a whistle. As dawn approaches, the birds pick up their songs and calls with gusto. For the half hour just before dawn, I give up listening for whistles because nothing can be heard over their loud chorus. I have never heard anything like it. It is as though the birds of the forest are trumpeting the arrival of some great king, the dawn, the day, the coming of the sun, worthy of all the noise and song that they are capable of making. Golly! They sure make a big deal about the new day, I think. I realize that I have never greeted a day in all my ten years the way that they do every morning. Shortly after this proclamation at dawn, Dad and Kara stir next to me. Still no whistles.

9 AM I JUST IMAGINING THINGS?

The morning is hard for me. I am exhausted from my night's vigil and a little disgusted with myself. I probably did just imagine the whole thing with the whistles and now I am so tired I don't even feel like hiking. Still, I help Dad pack up our gear and we start out on the trail. My grumpy mood infects Kara and she is also on edge, whining occasionally as we walk. To make matters worse, it suddenly starts to rain, a steady, foggy drizzle pouring down through the canopy. Dad hands me a poncho we brought along, but poor Kara just has to put up with a wet coat. She keeps shaking as we walk along through the rain.

Finally, around noon, Dad suggests that we take a break near a large group of rocks. One of them has an overhang that juts out a few feet and we are able to get at least a little shelter from the damp. We eat more energy bars and dried fruit.

"Let's rest for a bit and see if the rain clears. The rain has slowed us down some, but I would guess we have less than two hours before we reach the outpost. We can afford to wait a little bit," Dad says, stretching out against the gray rock. I am totally relieved. After a walk in the rain and my night of whistle-watch, I could really use a nap. I fall quickly asleep next to Kara.

When I wake up, the rain has cleared although the sky is still overcast.

"Looks like we've hit some luck! Let's start walking before it picks up again," Dad says. I feel much better after some rest and my head starts to clear. I am totally convinced now that I must have imagined those whistles. Besides, I now remember that old Juan Carlos had said you had to whistle back the tune for El Tunchi to come after you. I have no intention of whistling at all, so even if El Tunchi is real (which he probably isn't) I have nothing to worry about.

Just as I am opening my stride and

relaxing into this new revelation, I hear a sound that almost makes me trip and fall. It is coming from in front of me, a whistle in three tones. Goosebumps run up and down my spine as I stare out, trying to determine what is making the sound. Suddenly, I realize it is coming from right in front of me, repeating over and over again. The whistle is from Dad!

"Dad! What are you doing?" I ask, running up to him, my face pale.

"What? What do you mean?" Dad asks.

"You are whistling," I say. Dad frowns.

"Oh, am I? I guess it was unconscious. I've had this tune in my head the last couple of days and I just don't seem to be able to figure out where it's from." Dad stops talking as he sees the look on my face.

"You ... just ... whistled ... back," I say, emphasizing every word. Dad shakes his head.

"Now, Eli, I think we've had just about enough of this El Tunchi stuff. It is not real!" he says. Before he finishes speaking, however, there is a sudden movement in the underbrush to our right. Kara starts barking.

"Not real, huh?" I ask, turning towards the movement. Dad says nothing, but turns around as well. I don't know what to expect.

What will it look like? Will it be a man, tall and thin with long, white fingers which will grab me and Dad away into the forest? Or will it be just a shadow hunting us down through the jungle paths? I brace myself as the bushes part and out of them springs forth...

10 EL TUNCHI?

"A pig!" Dad says, a stunned look on his face. There standing before us is, indeed, just that, a pig or a peccary, to be exact. It's a wild hog that roams through the forest. It usually stays away from people, but somehow accidently stumbled upon Dad and Kara and me. Kara immediately barks at it, her hackles raised. The peccary takes one look at us and jumps, squealing in shock.

"Uh, oh! We've startled it," Dad says.

"*We* startled *it?*" I yell back. The air fills with a strong, musky smell almost like a skunk.

"Yep, there's the musk. Be careful, they can be dangerous when they feel threatened!" Dad says, spreading his arms out and stepping in front of me. The peccary shakes its head back and forth and begins to grunt at the ground. I notice the long, sharp canine teeth framing its mouth.

"Here it comes!" Dad says. The peccary charges. I fall down behind Dad and close my eyes, preparing for impact. But, no impact comes. Instead there is a growl and a snarl and a heavy thud. I open my eyes and see Kara on top of the peccary, a flash of grey fur and sharp teeth.

"Kara!" I yell, afraid that she will get hit by one of the peccary's teeth. Within moments, the fight is over and the peccary runs off into the rainforest, squealing and grunting, blood dripping from a bite on its side. Kara calmly sits down in front of Dad and me.

Collared Peccary - Pecari Tajacu

This guy was big and scared of us.
He left off a strong musk smell right
before he charged. Kara saved us!

rounded rump

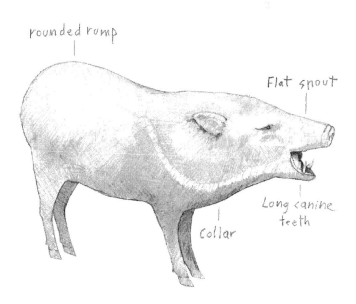

Flat snout

Long canine
teeth

Collar

"Good girl, Kara!" Dad says, coming to her and petting her. Both Dad and I spend a few minutes thanking Kara for probably saving our lives. She seems unharmed and unconcerned. She simply looks straight ahead, panting and then licks my face as if to say, "What is all the fuss about? This is, of course, what I am here for, to get the two of you out of trouble." We walk the last hour back to the outpost quickly. I make Dad promise not to whistle.

"Eli, you don't honestly think that the peccary came out of the jungle at us because of El Tunchi, do you?" he asks.

"Listen, all I know is that old Juan Carlos said if you whistle back then El Tunchi will either take you or terrorize you. I don't know about you, but I think one wild peccary is enough terror for one day," I say. Dad laughs, but does agree not to whistle, just in case.

We get back to the outpost around sunset and I have never been so glad to see other people in my life. I am even happy to see loud Mr. Johnson and old Juan Carlos. We were only in the rainforest for two days, but it feels like we have been gone for weeks. That night, lying underneath my mosquito net with Kara at my feet, I go over my field journal for the trip. I did pretty well for my first expedition. I was able to add four new species to my journal - the pink river dolphin, the blue morpho butterfly, the agouti, and, of course, the dwarf dragon lizard. I also make a quick sketch of the peccary and, just for my own satisfaction, I draw a spooky picture of a tall, pale man with long, white fingers standing in the forest and label it "El Tunchi". I close my book and fade into sleep.

As Dad, Eli, and Kara rest at the outpost, the clouds clear over the rainforest and the moon rises, full and bright. Under the leaves of the trees where the dark crouches in at the edges of the moonlight, a sound echoes through the forest, clear and low—a whistle in three tones.

El Tunchi

ABOUT THE AUTHOR

Anna Hagele has four kids and she spends much of her time going on pretend and real adventures with them. Just like Eli and his dad, she is an avid animal lover and likes to observe and learn about all of the animals she comes across. She hopes that her books will help kids to open their minds to all of the life around them and to awaken their adventurer spirits.

She lives with her husband, Michael, and their four children in Santa Fe, New Mexico.

Be the first to hear about Eli's next adventure, contests, giveaways, and more!

Join
whereselimoore.com

Like
facebook.com/whereselimoore

Follow
twitter.com/whereselimoore

35022952R00043

Made in the USA
Columbia, SC
19 November 2018